Christian Tho't

Ko.Co. Marx

DEDICATION

I dedicate this book to all women and men out there who have many struggles in life and feel that no one understands. This book is dedicated to those who suffer in silence yet still have the desire to make life work. This book serves the purpose to give you hope, a smile, and a chance to realize that someone understands you.

CONTENTS

ACKNOWLEDGMENTS

I would like to thank God for instilling me with the desire to write since I was a child. I thank him for allowing me this opportunity and for finally allowing me to see I am worthy enough to actually start. I would also like to thank my sister who is usually in the background encouraging me to follow my dreams. I would also like to thank a dear friend who encouraged me to follow my passions and dreams when I was in a dark place in my other career.

1 I'M A SAVAGE

"LET US SAY AMEN!" my homegirl yelled out loud as I told her about how I finally went to therapy for my food addiction. Sitting across from me was Ava, 5'4", light-skinned, kinky short hair, and overweight. She has been my best friend since our mothers were both pregnant with us. We are both twenty-nine, on the brink of thirty and we've definitely had our good times and bad times. "Girl, I'm just so happy I've finally taken that step; I don't know why people don't believe you can be addicted to food," I said. "Right, you can be addicted to sex, love, drugs, tv, an unproductive life, but somehow when it's food you're just considered a fat lazy bitch" she said. As soon as she said that, our church sister entered the restaurant. It was Sis. Beaumont, you know the loud ghetto educated heifer who always has her nose in somebody else's business except for her own husband's.... but yea, THAT sister! If you go to church, I'm sure you know at least one or two.

"TRACIE! TRACIE! TRACIE!" my friend was yelling at me and I finally snapped out of it, "WHA....," I stated as she interrupted me with, "Girl ain't that Sis. Beaumont from church, hell I'm about to hide and go to the bathroom" she said as she gets up and walks off to the bathroom before I could respond! Old heifer! Sure enough, Sis. Beaumont walks over to the booth. This was a loud ghetto church going woman. She fit the stereotype, big bootie and all. The biggest Christian of all. High heels, blonde hair, with a Mrs. Steal your man attitude. Now don't get me wrong, she wasn't ugly

1

externally but internally I'll have to take that one up with the Lord. She speaks to me "Hey Sis. Tracie, I saw Ava run off to the bathroom, how are you doing?" she asks as she leans in for a hug. Damn! Her breath STINKS. I truly hope this does not turn into a conversation… "How's the job coming along?" Damn, literally always in my business, I thought to myself.

"It's going good actually. How's Bro. Beaumont doing?" I asked. She gave me a look, then responded, "He's good." Was, "he's good," all she had to say? Hah! Asking about HER MAN worked to my advantage, she gave another hug and exited stage left to the take-out counter. Now, does it really take Ava that long to use the bathroom? She comes out, looking crazy and looking around to see if Sis. Beaumont was still in the restaurant. Then she sits down and gives me a funny look. "What?" I asked her. "Tracie, you won't believe this." "What girl?" Tell me!" She held her head down and looked me dead in my eyes when she said, "The church has caught fire!" "WHAT!" I yelled. Within about twenty minutes we were across the street from the church looking at what was left of it. My father, his father, and his father spent years to build this church and now nothing remains. I looked at the state of the church, the black smoke all around, the ashes flying in the air, and suddenly it was all too familiar.

Me and Ava parted ways after leaving the church and I came back home and did some cleaning. It was around 8pm when I received a text from the boo.

"I can't believe the church is gone! How's your dad handling it?
"About as well as can be expected. Earlier, when Ava and I stopped by to see what was left of the building, daddy and a few of the other brethren were standing

outside praying and I could've sworn I saw some tears come out of daddy's eyes."

I laid my head down on my pillow with a small sigh out loud thinking of life in general. About 30 seconds later, I got another text from him, "Wow. Have you talked to your mom? I know Bro. Jaxson said he was already looking for another building" he said. I replied immediately, "I haven't but I planned on stopping by there tomorrow. I'm about to get ready for bed. I'll talk to you later babe."

I placed my phone down, got up from the bed and walked to the bathroom to pee. After peeing, I washed my hands and stood there staring at myself in the mirror. I guess I wasn't too shabby. I stood about 5'7", natural medium brown hair, cinnamon colored skin, makeup less, big lips, big negro nose, and small ears. I wasn't ugly but I wasn't a looker either. I brushed my teeth, wrapped my hair up, placed my bonnet on, wiped my face, locked my apartment doors, turned all my lights out and went to bed. As I laid in bed, thoughts began to run rampant. From bills, to the church, to mom and dad, to Peter, my job, and everything else under the sun.

I eventually drifted off to sleep.

"BANG! BANG! BANG!"

"WTF is that noise!" I said to myself. I rolled over in bed scared as hell, grabbed my phone, saw 12:26AM. "BANG BANG BANG..."

It sounded too close for comfort; someone was knocking on my door.

My phone rings, I see its Peter! "Girl let me in! Don't you hear me out here knocking on yo' door!" I open the door shocked, with a confused look on my face "What are you doing here? You didn't tell me you were coming over and you do know I have work tomorrow, right?" I closed the door behind him as he walked in.

He leans right in and starts kissing me. This man was fine! I couldn't resist him. Tall, dark, and handsome, standing six feet two inches, dark chocolate skin, chest and abs ripped, curly black hair, with a perfectly trimmed goatee. To top it off he had on my favorite cologne, Polo Black.

He continued, ravenously kissing down my neck, slowly to my collar bone; before I knew it, my shirt was off exposing my breast. He pushed me up against the wall and licked down to my left breast while squeezing the other with his thick solid hand. This was it! Stick a fork in me, I was completely done! I had just vowed celibacy away from this man about a month ago! Down to the floor we both went as I unzipped his pants, pulled down his boxers, and guided him into me. "Oh my gosh, mmmmm Bro. Beaumont you feel so good." I dug my fingernails into his back and wrapped my legs tightly around his bottom, pulling him in closer. "Yes, yes that's it, right there baby, don't stop!" I moaned. He grunted as he continued to thrust into me passionately, "oh baby, I'm about to cum!" "Yes hunny, cum inside me, oh baby, cum Peter Beaumont, cum baby!" He loves it when I call his full name out when we're having sex. He's told me in the past that he thinks it makes him cum harder. He squeezes me as he lets go deep inside me and my body shudders into a million different little waves. We both lay there breathing, heart rates calming, with small beads of sweat dripping down our bodies. God forgive me, I think to myself. What am I doing? I'm not sure, but this man definitely knew how to fuck. I wonder if this is how he made love to Sis. Beaumont. Does he make her feel this way too?

2 BACKGROUND

I hate it here! You guessed it. I'm at my 9-5, miserable, working my ass off while at the same time getting a foot in the ass. These people don't appreciate anything I do and don't pay anything! I'm not sure why I even bothered getting my master's in public health; my salary increased a whopping $0.35! I've been working here for two years and I've gotten no promotion, just more work and responsibility. I check my email.

"The reports on contact tracing for Covid-19 have been compromised, please gather all information and re-submit by 3PM tomorrow. Thanks."

GREAT! How am I supposed to gather all this information in such a short amount of time and send it in by tomorrow?

I walk out of my office and take a right into Sharon's office. "Hey Sharon, do I need to call city hall and get all the tracing reports sent back to me from their contact tracing department; because otherwise I have no idea how I'm going to submit this information to the company by 3PM tomorrow!" I asked my boss.

"Yes, that's what you need to do. What happened to the files that were already sent to you?" she asked.

"They were compromised," I said with a sarcastic tone, while rolling my eyes. My boss just laughed as I walked away and went back to my office to make a phone call. It was a little after 12 right now, so I had time to eat a quick lunch and then call city hall to get all this information sent back to me.

I made sure to let them know, please add a BAA agreement and send it over a secure citrix server.

At around 4pm, I finally received all of the reports via a secure email connection this time! I'm so glad I got that over with today, because that's one less thing I have to worry about. My mind kept drifting back to last night and the way Peter was banging me. I started feeling him again in between my legs. You know how when the dick is good, you still feel him some hours or a day later? Phantom dick is what I call it; that is what's happening right now.

I finished up the rest of my work and left at around 5PM. I stopped to grab a bite to eat and called my mom to let her know I was on my way to check on her and dad.

"Hey mama, what you doing?" I asked. "Nothing child, just trying to finish cooking these oxtails so your sorry ass daddy can have something to eat, you know he act like he can't cook for his damn self" "Mm, hmm," I responded. She kept going, "Hell, I work every damn day. I'm a woman, I don't have any days off. Oh baby, I'm sorry, are you just getting off work?" she asked.

"Yes ma'am, I was calling to let you know I'm on my way over to check on you and daddy." "Oh ok, well come on, we're here. I'll see you in a bit." "All right, bye mama, love you." I hung up the phone, turned the radio up, and drove about ten more minutes to mama and daddy house.

I walked into the house and it smelled heavenly. "Hey

mama!" I gave her a hug and walked into the kitchen. Mama was sitting in her favorite black chair. "How you doing, sweetheart?" she asked. "I'm doing all right, how are you doing, and where is daddy?" "Oh, he's out there in the backyard child. I guess he'll be in here in a minute." "Ok then."

"So, how has daddy been since the church caught fire?"

"He's doing okay. He talked to Bro. Jaxson and they're trying to either find another building or some land to build the church on. He's just sad because you know that's his so-called legacy."

"Yes, ma'am I know. All he knows is church business. His life revolves around preaching, singing, teaching, and trying to organize church functions." I said. Daddy finally walks in the house and before I could speak to him, mama yells, "Rodney, wash your hands!" I just looked at daddy and said "Hey daddy" Daddy said, "Hey Tracie, how are you?" Daddy had this look of defeat and despair on his face. "I'm all right, just got off work and came over to check on you and mama."

"Oh ok, thank you daughter. Let me wash my hands and eat these oxtails that the HBIC cooked before it gets too late." I wanted to ask specifically about things regarding the church but I didn't want to pry too much. I also figured he would bring it up if he wanted to talk about it. I had a lot of questions to ask mama and daddy about what happened to the church but I would just wait and call mama to ask her later. I stayed a little while longer at my parents' house and then left. I was tired and besides I had to go to the store to pick up a few hair items before heading home.

While at the store, my phone rang. It was Sharon my

boss from work; I let the bitch go straight to voicemail. If it's important, she'll leave one. I got my hair items and headed home.

Overall, my life is a little boring. My life's focus has been solely on pleasing everyone around me which has often led to my being miserable. I was diagnosed with clinical depression at age eleven and that's more than likely how I developed my current food addition. I am an only child, but I do have a lot of cousins who I consider to be siblings to me, because we all grew up together. Arisa and James were my closest cousins growing up. They are fraternal twins sitting at thirty-three years old. Arisa is married to her high school sweetheart Billy and they have two children, Princess and Jacoby. James has a two-year-old a son, Trey, from a previous relationship, but is now engaged to his white fiance Sabrina.

I would on occasion hang out with them and their families but Covid-19 had other plans. My best friend Ava has been my rock. I'm thankful for her friendship. It's not often you find another woman who is a true friend, down for you and not secretly envious or jealous of you. Most women are usually always putting one another down or in competition with one another. She is genuinely one of the best people I have ever met and I'm blessed to have her. She has a boyfriend, Will, she's been dating since we were twenty-six, and he seems like a decent guy. Ava adores him and she seems happy.

I've been single, since the age of nineteen. I was in a physical and emotionally abusive relationship. No one knew, as I managed to hide it well. His name was Richard. Richard was Mexican, and it was the first time I dated outside my race. That was a mistake. Every time we disagreed; he'd jump at the chance of calling me the N word. I always thought that was rather peculiar considering he's a minority himself; but since he and his family spent their whole lives passing as white, it makes sense.

I try hard to think of any redeeming qualities that made me stay with him throughout part of my years in college. Maybe the fact that he was a hard worker. Besides that, he called me fat, ugly, pulled guns out on me, and treated me very poorly. That relationship left wounds that never healed and I'm still dealing with the repercussions of it to this day.

After things ended with Richard, I never had another serious relationship. They were all just a waste of time, effort, and energy. Nothing fruitful came from any of the men I was with. In the end, it only left me feeling used with a sense of hate and resentment inside of me towards men.

I grew up with a good father in the home, one would think my experience with men would be more positive. At twenty-seven, I believed I was in a relationship with another guy. About five months into what I thought was "dating," I found out he was married. This guy was also sexually coercive. He treaded a thin yet ambiguous line between rape and sexual coercion. We kept having sex (off and on) for a couple years after I found out his marital status. There were numerous times, I'd say "NO!" but he still found a way to force himself inside me. Whether that came through forcing my legs apart, pinning my hands down behind me, or even using his legs in my side to make me stay in place; but for some reason it wasn't enough for me to end it. If you're reading this, please keep in mind that just because a woman gets wet; she does not always want to have sex with you! I eventually had the courage to end it for good and it was one of best decisions I ever made. Throughout all this time, school had been my best friend. My first degree was a bachelor's of science in Biochemistry, obtained a certificate as a medical laboratory science assistant, and then later went back to school to get my master's in public health.

All of this, to end up working in an office, making less than $70,000/year. These degrees did not get me a six-figure salary, but rather a six-figure debt.

Growing up, I went to church every Sunday. My dad was a deacon at the church and he took it very seriously. My going to church continued into adulthood when I moved out, but nothing changed in my life. I was only checking the box and truth be told, it seemed the more I went to church, the more I felt boxed in and restricted. All my life, I kept hearing about how everything is a sin and wrong, but the freedom in Jesus was rarely ever discussed. Despite that, I knew God was real. God was someone I knew I never wanted to turn my back on.

I've been in therapy about two months for my food addiction. It has helped some. I'm able to choose healthier resources when I'm feeling down instead of running to food. It used to be so bad that I would cry while eating two pints of mint chocolate chip ice cream and then lay in bed right afterwards. Now, I'm down to one pint! I am also taking my depression medication less often. Look at that progress, nothing but God!

I grabbed my phone. I guess I wasn't important today because my phone was dry. Sharon hadn't left a voicemail and I haven't heard anything from Peter! Ava hadn't even texted or called. I browsed around on my social media accounts for a little while. There was this new one called Facehooked and it's funny because I often found my face hooked to it. I had quite a few friends on there and would spend a lot of time scrolling through the feed. I would laugh at the occasional meme and marvel at how everyone's life seemed so perfect. Everyone had it all together. Perfect marriage, perfect homes, perfect careers and families, and was always smiling.

A part of me loved to see it but another part of me questioned if it was reality.

I logged off Facehooked, turned on the TV and went to the kitchen. Ended up grabbing some leftover chili to eat. Warmed up my food, grabbed myself a strawberry wine cooler out the fridge and plopped down on the couch right in front of the TV.

"Jamal Turner, 42-year-old black man shot and killed today by police in New Jersey after running to save a child from a vicious German Shepard barking and running towards the child," the story continued, "Local witnesses say the man was seen casually walking in the neighborhood when he heard a child screaming for help and started to run towards the child. Sources say, "an anonymous person made a phone call to police saying a suspicious man was attacking a dog and a child in the neighborhood." The reporter continued "the city is now in turmoil as the protests have already started, as local authorities gather more evidence, we hope to know more later on this story."

I turned off the TV. The news exhausted me. I'm so glad I have tomorrow off. I needed the weekend. I was tired.

3 FOR REAL

"OMG, OMG, OMG, yes, yes, yes, eat this pussy baby!" I moaned as I grinded my hips up into his face. He gripped my hips and held me down tightly as I orgasmed my wetness all over his face.

"Damn baby, you taste so good." Peter said. It was about 6:00PM. Now, I know what you're thinking. What does Peter do that he always has time to be with you AND his wife. Did I also mention he and his wife have two kids? Peter AKA Bro. Beaumont worked as a stock and forex trader. He could work anywhere as long as he had access to a phone or a computer. His wife, Sis. Rosie Beaumont was a full-time school teacher and their kids were at school. We would usually mess around at this time., and that's why I was surprised when he showed up at my door so late the other morning. I didn't ask any questions though. Believe it or not, we did not hook up often, maybe once or twice every two weeks.

I smiled and said "I guess I do," as he climbed on top of me and kissed me with all my juices still fresh in his mouth and on his lips. "Peter, do you ever feel...well...I don't know?" I asked. He hesitated because he already knew where I was going with this. I would often bring this up during our rendezvous. Even though this had been going on between us for a while, I had been feeling more guilty and regretful. I was also getting a little tired of this being all there is for me.

"We are just having a good time. You know the situation. Let's not think too much about it." he said.

"All right, get up, put your clothes on!" I said feistily. He started looking confused. "What's the problem this time?" He asked.

"Nothing, I just want you to go. Like leave for real, NOW!" I got louder.

I hopped out of bed and started helping him get his stuff faster. "You done lost it and you have issues," he exclaimed. "Yea I do, now you got less than a minute to get your black ass out of here expeditiously!"

He started walking towards the door. I was already standing there with the door open waiting for him to walk out. He stepped out and I immediately closed the door behind him with no other words exchanged. "Good riddance!" I uttered to myself after I shut the door. For some reason I was proud of myself. So, I went to bathe and hit up Alexa. "Alexa, play *Freak Hoe* by Future." I turned the music up loud as hell and danced all around. I was feeling myself!

I finally sat down after dancing for about an hour. Got on Facehooked and read the first status that popped up on my news feed.

"I just want to thank everyone who has been solid in my life. Most of you know I usually don't put my personal business on a platform like this, but a lot of people have asked me questions, so I feel I should address this once and for all. When we first got married, I knew that my husband had been battling some issues. For all those saying, I should have paid attention before we got married, I did not see this beforehand. In case you've heard the gossip, yes, my husband has expressed to me that he is homosexual and he has feelings for men. Of course, after learning this information I have taken several steps to ensure my physical and mental health. For those who love and care about me, I would like you all to know that I am fine. My husband and I have agreed to work through our issues and like the vows say for better or for worse. God will be on our side and will help us get through this. Thanks for all the calls, texts, and well wishes." -Mrs. Rosie B.

My mouth dropped wide open. What the hell did I just read? Is this a joke or some shit? She can't be referring to Peter, the man that just left here. There is just no way. Why would she post this on social media? I immediately picked up the phone and called Ava, "WTF is Sis. Beaumont's post about?" I asked!

"I SAW THAT! Girl I can't believe she put all that out there like that. So apparently, Peter is gay. That can't be real!" She responded.

Now, I can't say too much. Although Ava is my best friend, she did not know I was fucking him. She thought I been talking to John. That's another story.

Ava continued, "Did you see his sister comment on the post girl? In the comments section she asked Rosie to please take the post down."

I blinked twice. I had to tell her. I couldn't hold it anymore.

"I was fucking him Ava." I said short, quick, and snappy. There was a long yet brief pause on the phone. I could tell Ava did not know how to respond to what she'd just heard me say.

"Come again," she said.

"I was fucking, Peter fucking Beaumont!" I said louder.

"I'm at work girl, I have to go." Ava responded as she hung up the phone. She sounded perplexed and disappointed all in one. Damn, was she mad or something? Of course, you know the next person I called on the phone.

Peter didn't answer. I kept calling. Finally, on the sixth try, I got an answer.

"Peter, WTF! Are you kidding me? You gay or some shit?" I yelled on the phone.

"Look, you're like the one-hundredth person calling me about what Rosie has posted on Facehooked. That shit is fake and she's trying to cover her ass and ruin my entire reputation. She has taken the kids and left!"

"So, YOU GAY??" I asked again more direct.

"No, Tracie. I am NOT gay! And if I was, would that be a problem for you miss homophobic? Anyway, I don't even know what Rosie's motive is for posting that shit on Facehooked."

"So, you out here like that? Fucking me, your wife, and men? Community dick and all!" I said again, totally ignoring the fact that he said he wasn't gay and called me homophobic.

"I told you the truth, now bye bye. My folks calling me and then people at church calling me. I have no more time for extra drama!" He said as he hung up the phone in my face.

I could not believe this shit. What would prompt Sis. Beaumont to just go off like this and then on a public platform if there was absolutely no truth to it? Now I needed to go get tested! I should've been doing that but obviously a man like Peter is not to be trusted. "FUCK!" I yelled out loud to myself as I threw the phone to the floor.

Breathe, Breathe, Breathe! I went to pick up my phone from the floor. Since, it was the weekend, I scheduled an online appointment with my OB-GYN next Tuesday at 10:30AM. Thank God that time slot was open! I needed to get full panel STD testing after this news. This is what I get! I have fallen away from God so much and look at how my life is turning out. A hot mess! God forgive me and just take care of me! That's all I could say.

My phone rang. Before I could even say hello, mama started in "Hey child, did you hear about what happened between Bro. and Sis Beaumont at church? Now why would she put their business out there like that on social media and on Face-shooked at that?"

"You mean Facehooked mama? Anyway, yes, I heard. This is just all too much. I can't believe it at all." Now of course nobody knew Peter and I were sleeping together. Not even Ava knew before I just told her. For all I know she was pissed at me for not telling her. Mama started again, "Yea, I hope Sis. Rosie goes to get tested as soon as possible. These men don't care out here, they are just plain nasty. Raw dogging everything and everybody for a nut!"

This is just how mama is. She speaks her mind and holds nothing back. A true woman of God, will do anything for you, but will not bite her tongue.

"Yes ma'am!" That's all I could respond with at the moment. I was processing my own feelings and thoughts about this entire situation and did not know what to feel.

I changed the subject. "So, since the church building is down, where are we having church tomorrow? I haven't heard anything from anyone yet."

"Sis.Penny said she would send out a group text and let everyone know we would meet on a video platform tomorrow for church." Mama said.

"Oh ok. I mean, I guess that's good. It's sad though because we had just recently got back used to going to the building because of COVID-19, it feels like we're going backwards." I said.

"Anyway girl, let me get off this phone. I'm trying to work on something for my grandbabies, Jacoby and Princess for tomorrow." Mama refers to Jacoby, Princess, and Trey sometimes as her grandkids because I was her only child and did not have any kids. Luckily, mama has not pressured me to have children. She and daddy seem to want me to have a productive and fulfilled life first.

"Ok I said, I'll see y'all on video I guess tomorrow then." I said.

"Yea, and don't forget to pray for Bro. and Sis. Beaumont and their kids. They truly need our prayers right now." She said.

"Yes ma'am. Good day, love you." I hung up the phone. Whew this was a lot to process. Then church tomorrow on video. This is too much.

I called mama back right quick. She answered, "Hey mama, I forgot to ask you, did the police ever investigate the fire at the church. Has there been any leads on how it started?"

"Well, your daddy said the firemen did not believe the origin stemmed from anyone setting the fire and that it may have been electrical in nature."

"Hmm, I said. Ok, I was just asking because I hadn't heard anything."

"Yea, you know the women of the church are always in the dark. The men don't share much of anything, but expect us to contribute." she said.

"I know mama, anyway ok, love you again and talk later."

"Love you too Tracie" mama said as she hung up the phone.

I couldn't believe all this was happening. I thought I would be able to actually chill this weekend. I could go to the store and get the rapid HIV testing, but I would just wait to go to the doctor Tuesday to get blood tested. Did Sis. Beaumont know about Peter and me? What if the whole entire church finds out? Right now, the focus is on Peter, but he could expose me any minute. How would that make mama and daddy feel? My phone dinged; it was the text message from Sis. Penny with access for the video call to church tomorrow.

I got up from the couch and threw on some shorts and

a t-shirt. I figured I would head to the park. I needed to clear my head and a walk in the park is what I would have to settle for.

4 UP IN DIS CHURCH

"Good Morning Everyone! Thank you all for joining us on this platform. As you all know there was an incident at the church building causing a fire and we haven't quite figured out a place for us to have worship yet." Bro. Jaxson started.

He continued, "So from this Sunday on, we will be having church on this video platform called Voom. Remember, we are missionaries for Christ, that is why we are called Greater Hope Missionary Baptist Church!"

While he was talking, I was browsing to see who all was online. Seemed like most people who usually came to church were on Voom. Of course, Sis. Beaumont was not and neither was Peter. This whole concept was very interesting and I had no idea how this would continue to work. Most of us black people thrived on being able to meet in person weekly. It was nothing like hearing everyone sing along with the piano, drums, and guitar. No way we could have all that on Voom without the frequencies interfering and becoming too much. Everyone was on mute; some had their videos on and some did not.

Bro Jaxson continued, "As we prepare for our order of service and figure things out, please enjoy our first song." Bro. Jaxson started playing the song "Pass me not" over his computer speaker. It sounded muffled and horrible.

I started wondering if anyone was going to say anything about the drama that happened between the Beaumont's but hopefully not. As the music was playing, I scrolled through the participants and saw Sis. Jaxson on video eating a fried chicken leg. I chuckled out loud to myself.

Finally, the music was over and Bro. Jaxson comes back.

"If anyone needs prayer, we will use the next minute to accept prayer requests through chat or unmute and request."

Bro. Rowe in the chat box:

"Please pray for my son, he's working as a travel nurse in the ICU in New York right now and just tested positive for Covid-19. Prayers for his health and to keep him safe."

Sis. Ashely over voice:

"I'm asking for prayers for my child's father. He done got locked up again and I'm just asking for prayers that God work in his life."

Sis. Rodney over voice:

"Yes, continue to keep the Beaumont's in your prayers please. They are going through a tough time right now. Prayers for their emotional and physical health during this time."

Did mama really have to ask for prayers for the Beaumont's? She truly gets on my nerves. Someone unmuted and said, "AMEN!"

Bro Jaxson, came back on," Let us pray."
Bro Jaxson started the prayer and it lasted for about ten minutes. I ended up falling asleep for a second.

To make a long story short, they explained how they would be doing offering from now on. How long we would be on Voom, and where they are in the process of finding somewhere to worship.

Bro. Ramone preached the sermon for this Voom service. He used Matthew 10:1-15 for his message.

Voom service started at 10AM and ended at 11:45AM. It was a lot shorter than what it was when we actually went to church. I actually enjoyed it and the scripture made a lot of sense. I figured I would probably read it again tonight before going to bed.

Ava ended up coming over to the apartment after church service. We discussed how she didn't know I was sleeping with Bro Beaumont. She seemed disappointed in me but she did not judge me. All she said was that I should go and get checked out to make sure I was ok.

After she left, I took a nap. I was extremely exhausted and I was not looking forward to going to work tomorrow. I woke up, went to go pee and came back to look at my phone. Dry again. So, I called John.

"Hey girl, what's up? He asked.

"Just trying to relax and take my mind off my crappy life, want to go grab a bite to eat at around like 3:30PM?" I asked him.

"Sure, want me to come pick you up, or want to meet there?" He asked. "I'll meet you there, I have to go put some gas in my car. Let's meet at Olive Garden for 3:45." I said.

"Aight, see you then." He hung up the phone.

Even though I did not consider this a date by any means, I figured I would dress rather cute. I put on my long curly blonde wig, placed on some light foundational makeup, and some matte nude lip gloss.
I also made sure to put on some cute little hoop earrings. I chose a fitted V-neck top to highlight my boobs and some jeans which highlighted my figure and round bottom.

John and I met at the restaurant. I saw him get out of the car. He was this nerdy black guy, but cute nonetheless. He owned his own local tech company in town. He does not have any kids and last time we met he wasn't seriously dating anyone. We met about two years ago through one of Ava's co-workers at a Christmas party. I had friend zoned him immediately, he just wasn't it for me.

He was single and about 5'9", real light skinned, reddish hair, and wore glasses. Picture a shorter and less muscular Michael Ealy. He walked over to my vehicle.

"Hey girl," he said as he reached to give me a hug. "Back up playa, you know this virus ain't playing with nobody," I said jokingly.

We both laughed and entered the restaurant and eventually ended up seated after about 10 minutes. The waiter came over and took our orders.

"So, how have you been Tracie. What's been going on with you? It has to be something considering you invited me out to lunch!"

"Whatever John! I've been okay, just trying to figure out where my life is headed. I feel like I'm being pulled in a million different directions, and I'm failing at every single point." I started shaking my head.

John was just sitting there staring at me intensely as I talked. I wondered what he was thinking. He probably thought I was a fool.

"I understand dear. What is something that you really want to do with your life? What are you passionate about?" He asked.

"Honestly, I want to be a singer. I don't have the best voice in the world and I wouldn't be doing Christian music. You know my parents and everyone else would only expect gospel from me." The waiter brought our drinks and the salad. I always liked extra cheese. Then I ordered my food, lasagna and John ordered chicken parmesan.

"A singer huh? Well have you tried reaching out to anyone or posting videos of yourself singing on social media or anything?"

"No, I haven't. You know, singing won't pay the bills. If my songs aren't about shaking ass or swallowing, I will hardly get any air play time."

"Yea, you right about that one," he laughed.
"Well do you need any help, any money, or is there anything I can help you with?" he asked.

Damn. He instantly started looking a little cuter. He offered to help me. A man offered to help me! Wow!

"No, I'm fine. I have everything under control." I lied.

"If you have everything under control then why are you here with me, telling me your life is going in too many different directions?"

He had a point and I didn't know how to respond. "I just need to do something different. We used to hang out quite a bit and I haven't spoken to you in a while. Is there anyone new in your life?" I asked in an attempt to change the subject, but also genuinely curious.

"Not at the moment. I was having a casual relationship with someone I met from POF but things ended badly. I'm just ready to give my heart to one woman and settle down. I just can't find her." He said as he looked me directly into my eyes.

"That's unfortunate." I said coyly. The waiter had finally brought the food out to the table.

I said my grace over my own food individually but I noticed John just dug right in.

"Did you say grace?" I asked him.

"Wow, so you're analyzing me like that huh?" he joked.

"Yes, I am." I responded.
"God is great, God is good, and I think him for this food. Bow my head must we be fed, give us Lord our daily bread. Amen!"
"Ummmm, you know you just completely messed that up right?"
"Yepp!" He said
We both started laughing so hard. One of my guilty pleasures is watching people while they eat. I looked at the way he cut his chicken, it was very direct and straight to the point. He also cut his spaghetti up and

instead of twirling it around his fork to eat it, he would just stab it with the fork and eat it. Very peculiar guy. In a weird way, I guessed I liked it. He paid for our food. We finished and continued the small talk.

He walked me out to my car, and we continued conversing.

"Thanks Tracie, it was nice getting out of the house, even if I did have to pay for it!" He laughed. I could tell he was joking.

"Boy please! Ain't nobody ask you to pay. I'm an independent woman, I got me!" I retorted, while patting my chest.

"I know you got you, that's why I came to dinner with you."

"What you mean by that?" I asked

"You know me, I'm boring. If I'm not at work or spending time with my niece and nephews, I'm at home, that's what I mean"

"Huh? I still don't get what you mean?" I had this confused look on my face.

He steps a little closer to me and looks me in my eyes.

"What I mean is, I want to have you. And I don't mean that in a sexual way at all. You said you got you, let me have you. Let me be more than just, well this."

I couldn't believe what I was hearing. My life is out of control and here he is trying to make a move again. All I wanted to do was get out of the house and do something to take my mind off the drama. Here he is bringing more!

I didn't even know how to respond.

"Heh, John. I'm tired. Thanks for coming out to dinner. I'll talk to you later okay." He stood there looking confused as I popped open my door and got in. He just looked at me as he finally began to walk towards his car. I pulled out of the parking spot and honked my horn bye.

5 BACKFIRED

Yesterday at work had been an emotional roller coaster. I had a presentation to do in front of Portland Medical Center's CEO, Dr. Michael Divelo and six other hospital administrators. This presentation included ideas, strategies, and ways to help prevent and minimize spread of Covid-19 along with any other diseases. Most people said the presentation went well and they would contact me if they considered implementing any of my ideas at their hospital.

During my presentation yesterday, I felt weird. Like I couldn't remember what I was saying and like I was out of my body. However, today is a new day and I'm ready to take it on!

I told Sharon yesterday that I needed to leave for a doctor's appointment today and that I would return later. I left my job at around 9:45AM to make sure I got to the doctor on time.

I get there, fill out the paperwork and I'm sitting in the lobby. I'm nervous because I'm literally only here to get blood tested for STDs. My doctor is going to think I'm a whore. I've literally only been sleeping with one man; but it may have been two or three men based on Peter's nasty ass.

"Tracie!" the nurse calls out my name and I head to the back. "Date of birth" she says. "06/04/1991" I responded. The next part was the part I hated once I entered the room. Stepping on the scale. I stepped on the scale and to my surprise I had lost 5 lbs. I was excited for the small victories. "So, what are we seeing you for today?" she asked.

"Just my annual and I'd also like to get full panel STD testing please."

"Ok, got it."

"Are you taking any new medications outside of your birth control, depression meds, and ibuprofen for pain?" She asked.

"No ma'am" I answered.

She proceeded to ask a few more questions, get my vitals, and then stepped out of the room. Now it was playing the waiting game until the doctor finally entered the room. I checked my phone as usual and saw a text from Ava. "Call me when you get off work today." I just responded with "Ok."

I get on Facehooked and I see nothing out of the ordinary. A few more of my classmates from my masters' course getting engaged, or finding out their expecting, or buying a new home. A few other posts speaking of graduations or the occasional meme. Luckily, I did not see that someone passed away or had been killed. I find it odd that I keep getting on Facehooked expecting to see something different, when it's always the exact same.

Knock Knock! The doctor opens the door and I close my phone and set it to the side.

"Hi Tracie! How are you?" doc asked.

"I'm fine just here for my annual checkup and to get full panel std testing."

"Ok, good. Well, you know the routine. I'm going to ask you to get undressed and put on a gown and we'll come back in."

"Yes ma'am." I said.

Before she stepped out. She listened to my heart and lung sounds and walked out.

I hopped off the examination table, stripped, and put on that dreadful hospital gown.

A minute later the doctor and a nurse came in. You know what's next. Feet up in the stirrups, uncomfortable feeling, and you're done.

"Ok Tracie, I just took a sample swab from your cervix, Megan the nurse will be back in with your lab sheet for you."

"Ok, thank you." I said. The doctor washed her hands and left out of the room.

A few seconds later, Megan comes into the room. "Ok Tracie, take this to the lab to get them to draw your blood. We should have the results of your papsmear by the end of this week or early next week."

"Ok thank you."

"Go ahead and get dressed. The lab is down the hall to your right. You have a good day!" said Megan

I got dressed and immediately walked down the hall to the lab. That part didn't take long but I absolutely hated needles.

I left the lab and looked down at my phone.
It was heading towards twelve o' clock.

I figured I should get something to eat before heading back to work. I stopped by Whataburger and got a double meat Whataburger meal, whatasized, and an apple pie to go with it. I was hungry! Now how the heck, did I lose weight eating the way I do, I thought to myself.

If I had been trying to lose weight, trust me I wouldn't have. I got back to work stuffed but it felt good. I went back to my desk and saw a note that said, "Call me," - Sharon.

Oh Lord. What did I do now? I thought to myself. I picked up my office phone and called Sharon, although I could've easily just walked to her office.

"Tracie! The hospital (PMC) decided to implement your strategy on minimizing the spread of Covid-19! This is great!" she sounded so excited. I was actually shocked; this was probably the most exciting news I'd gotten lately.

"REALLY!! WOW! They decided fast. I just made the presentation on yesterday. Did they say why they chose it?" I asked.

"No, they didn't say but I'm just glad they did. This looks really great for our company. Do you know how many other hospitals, clinics, city officials, are now going to reach out to us!" she continued, "You have to let me do something nice for you soon!"

"No, no its ok Sharon! It's just my job." I responded.

"How'd your doctor's appointment go? Are you okay?" she asked.

"Uh yes, ma'am I'm fine. Thanks for asking. I better get to work on this presentation I have next week at UP." I said, trying to hurry off the phone.

"Ok! Congratulations Tracie! I'm proud of you!"

"Thank you so much! I'll see you later." I hung up the phone.

Wow that was really good news! Do I get a raise though? No! So, I'm really not that excited. I'm used to this, I do the work, Sharon gets the credit, and the cycle repeats. I sighed to myself, rolled my eyes, and started on my presentation for the biology department at UP. This presentation would be on transmission of Hep A in third world countries and how could we help minimize the spread and mitigate the severity of the disease in remote populations in third world countries.

I finally arrived home after a long day of work. All I wanted to do was crash! I took my shower and asked Alexa to play "Falling Short by Låpsley."

"Playing Falling Short by Låpsley," Alexa said. While the music played, I just laid across my bed. Once again, I'm in my thoughts and in my head. I guess this is all for my life. I'm not doing something I love; I have no man, I'm barely making ends meet, and church sucks! I turned off the music. I got off my bed and down on my knees.

Dear God,

Forgive me. I have sinned over and over again against your will. I've been sleeping with a married man and my life just sucks. I'm unhappy God. I've been unhappy for a very long time. Since a kid, when I was diagnosed with depression. What's wrong with me? Why do I seem to just love misery? Why do I always feel so stressed and boxed in? Thank you, God, for life and for my family. I am blessed, but how do I heal. How do I right, my wrongs? I'm just so messed up. I do want what they all have. A family, a bright future, to be happy. But if that's not the life you want for me God, please just let me know. Should I give more? Should I pray more? I'm just all confused and nothing is adding up. I'm asking for guidance, for deliverance, for peace...."

Bzzzz Bzzzzz Bzzzz, my phone starts vibrating in the middle of my prayer. I keep praying and ignore it. Eventually it stopped.

"God, I'm broken. Am I weak? Do I not trust you God? What could I......"?

Bzzzzz Bzzzz Bzzzzz the phone vibrates again. In the middle of my prayer, I open my eyes and look at my phone. It was Ava! Oh shoot, I forgot to call her.

"What could I...... no, how can I make this right? In Jesus' name I do pray, Amen."

I got off my knees and rang Ava back. She picked up on the first ring.

"Hey girl, what's going on?" I asked her with a bit of concern in my voice.

"I'm HIV+" Ava said.

I just sat on the phone. I had no idea what to say. There was silence for an entire minute.

34

"Ava… um, what…umm?" I stuttered.

"I have HIV Tracie, I found out the day you called me and told me about you and Peter."

"Huh…I'm so sorry Ava. I don't know what to…"

"Don't say anything. Have you gotten tested?" she asked.

"Yea… I went to the doctor today and they did bloodwork. I'll know later this week hopefully…. Why?"

"Will, he gave it to me." Ava said as she started crying. She continued, I'm having a hard time making out what she's saying, "Will he… I never would've thought Tracie… he…said he didn't know."

I'm staring at the ceiling in disbelief at what I'm hearing right now. I don't even know how to help my poor friend.

"When did he find out Ava, I'm just."

"Tracie, Will said he had been seeing Peter."

No way. Fuck me. This can't be. This can't be!

Ava continued, "That's why when you told me you were sleeping with Peter, I had to get off the phone, I did not know how to respond."

Oh my God! This can't be real life. At this point my life just has to be a movie.
"Ava, how can Peter be having sex with this many people. Is this real?"

"Yes, Tracie this is real," she said still crying.

"That's why I told you to make sure you get tested. I just can't do this anymore Tracie. I go to church, I treat people right, I mind my own business, and this is what I get as a result, HIV, huh?" she starts screaming. "HIV in the middle of COVID-19 huh TRACIE!!"

I'm literally on the phone silent with tears rolling down my eyes. Does life ever get better?

Ava continued, "I was in a relationship with Will, being faithful to Will, sleeping with one man, believing he was faithful, and now I'm fucked up for life because he's on the down low, sleeping with another down low ass nigga from church!" She yelled in my ear, "WTF kind of shit is this Tracie!"

"And to say I thought he was going to propose..." Ava said

I'm still silent. I'm trying to figure out how to process all this.

Anyway, she says, "I have to go. I just wanted to let you know. Don't say anything to me about Will anymore. Ever again. He's dead to me."

All I could utter was, "Ok. Look Ava, I'm so sorry. Let me know if there is anything, I can do..."

"There isn't" Ava said still crying, she continued "I have to go now." She hung up the phone before I could say anything else.
Holy sweet mother of Jesus! I said out loud to myself. Wow! Lord, I give up. I turn it over to you. Did I just get my answer to my own blood work as well? I may

as well prepare myself.

My best friend is now HIV+ because of a man she trusted and believed to be the one for her. I just can't anymore. I understand we're not supposed to have sex outside of marriage; but we're adults and we do have the urges. What are we supposed to do? Still get married even though we're broke and can't afford anything? Life is confusing, make it make sense. I just need this entire year to be over with.

I didn't know what do. I just needed silence. I locked up the apartment. Turned off the bedroom light and climbed into bed.

One day later....

The call from the doctor's office couldn't get here fast enough. That's all I've been thinking about since yesterday. I can't even focus on work. I hadn't heard anything from Ava since yesterday and I haven't tried to reach out. I'm not sure what to do. I'll probably reach out to her after I get my results. I'm just so nervous all I wanted to do was throw up.

All this stress had me feeling sick. Hopefully, I don't have the virus, covid to be specific. I'm going downstairs to get rapid tested today at lunch.

I worked on my presentation for UP most of the morning, checked my emails, and continued to collect and email the contact tracing information. I didn't even bring lunch today; I didn't feel like eating.

I headed downstairs and got the rapid testing done. Luckily, it's free for everyone who works here. I waited for about five minutes, and my result were negative. Praise God! At least one set of good news.

As soon as the clock hit 4:30PM, I was out the door!

I was ready to go and all I could feel was anxiety every second and minute of each and every hour. All I wanted to do was get home and in my bed!

Thursday

I was sitting at my desk when I got the call from the doctor's office. I didn't answer and they left a voicemail. I didn't know if I had the mental capacity to call back and get my results today while at work. I walked over to Sharon's office, "Hey Sharon, I may have to leave at around 12 today, something serious came up. Plus, I'm able to work from home."

"Ok girlfriend, I trust you! Afterall, I still owe you for PMC!" She said shaking in her chair excitedly. She is so silly sometimes.

I left out of her office and finished up a few things before leaving. I walked down to my car and listened to the voicemail.

"Miss Rodney, this is Shea at OB-GYN specialists calling with your recent lab results, please give us a call back."

I'm literally sitting in the car shaking. I can't do this. I can't call back! Oh God please! I dial the number slowly.
"Shea OB-GYN specialists how may I help you?"

"Yes, my name is Tracie Rodney, and I'm calling

Megan the nurse to get my results from my labs."

"Ok Tracie, just one moment." The music plays in the background.

"Hello Tracie, this is Megan Dr. Manner's nurse calling you with your recent lab results." She said

"Yes ma'am" I said.

"Um, we're going to need you to schedule a follow up appointment one day next week so that the doctor can discuss some things with you." She said.

I was nervous as all hell. Why hasn't she just told me the results of my lab work. My stomach is in knots and I feel like I have to shit on myself.

"Yes ma'am, I understand but can you just give my lab results to me right now over the phone." I asked.

"I can ma'am but first let me get you scheduled for one day next week. How does next Wednesday at 2:30pm work?" the nurse said.

"Um, sounds fine, I guess. What's going on? Do I have an STD or what?" I asked anxiously.

"Your blood work came back positive for pregnancy. You're pregnant. All your STD results came back negative."

I clutched my chest and took a deep breath in. Tears of sadness in my eyes. "Ma'am, that just can't be, I…there's no way I…"
"Miss Rodney, we'll see you next week. In the meantime, stay away from alcohol, ibuprofen, and away from smokers. Do not smoke anything yourself. We will call

you when we get your results back from your papsmear" the nurse said.

"Yes., uh, ok. Thank you. Have a nice day."

My life is over.

ABOUT THE AUTHOR

The author is literally from everywhere south. Born and raised in Louisiana but has lived in nearly every southern state for some time. The author of this book has always had a passion for writing but has only recently put pen to paper in hopes that their wild imagination is what someone else would crave to read. The author has a realistic mindset with a hint of cynicism, skepticism, and a dark naughty side. The author has a Christian background but the books are not limited to only holy speak. The author seeks to highlight and reveal the duality most Christians face, but never publicly speak about. The author wants to highlight their shadow self in the books as a way to make others feel comfortable doing the same. The author seeks to promote healing with the awareness that you are not alone. This is the authors first book of many to come and they pray you enjoy it.